Mrs. McBee
Leaves Room 3

To Susan Champion, who left us all too soon —G. B. M

To my grandmother, whom I love very much —G. Z.

Ω

Published by
PEACHTREE PUBLISHERS
1700 Chattahoochee Avenue
Atlanta, Georgia 30318-2112
www.peachtree-online.com

Edited by Kathy Landwehr
Design by Nicola Simmonds Carmack
The illustrations were created in acrylic and gouache on paper.

Printed in October 2016 by Tien Wah Press in Malaysia
10 9 8 7 6 5 4 3 2 1
First Edition

Library of Congress Cataloging-in-Publication Data

Names: McLellan, Gretchen Brandenburg, author. | Zong, Grace, illustrator.
Title: Mrs. McBee leaves room 3 / written by Gretchen Brandenburg McLellan;
illustrated by Grace Zong.
Description: First Edition. | Atlanta, Georgia : Peachtree Publishers, [2017] |
Summary: At the end of the school year, the children of Room 3 and Mrs. McBee
find their own ways of helping each other get ready to leave and say good-bye.
Identifiers: LCCN 2016020429 | ISBN 9781561459445
Subjects: | CYAC: Schools—Fiction. | Teacher-student relationships—Fiction. |
Farewells—Fiction.
Classification: LCC PZ7.1.M4627 Le 2017 | DDC [E]—dc23 LC record available
at *https://lccn.loc.gov/2016020429*

Mrs. McBee Leaves Room 3

Written by
Gretchen
Brandenburg McLellan

Illustrated by
Grace Zong

PEACHTREE
ATLANTA

A great sigh from Room 3 echoed down the halls of Mayflower Elementary.

"They heard," said the principal.

"They heard," said the custodian.

"They heard," said the lunch ladies.

Mrs. McBee had just told her class that she would not be returning to school after summer vacation.

"But you won't get to see me again!" said Jamaika.

"Or hear me read," said Max.

"Or see how much bigger I grew," said Lou.

"You can't go!" William said. "Nothing will ever be the same without you."

"I won't be far away," said Mrs. McBee. "But now it's time to squeaky-clean your desks and get the rest of the room ready too."

"Ready for what?" Flora asked.

"For our time together to end," said Mrs. McBee.

"What can we do?" Jamaika asked.

Mrs. McBee dragged a lumpy bag to the front of the room. Things clattered as she fished around inside. She pulled out a clipboard.

"What else is in there?" Jamaika asked.

"Hard hats and other surprises," said Mrs. McBee. "But before I show you, I need construction experts, librarians, packers, spellers, movers, and animal experts too. Maybe they can find the missing library mouse."

Mrs. McBee's eyes twinkled. "Will you help me?"

Everyone nodded.

Everyone except William.

"Who wants to be my assistant?" Mrs. McBee asked.

"I do!" Jamaika said.

Mrs. McBee passed her the clipboard and Jamaika signed up everyone for a team.

Everyone except William, who sat with his chin on his knees in the thinking corner.

The teams got to work.

The construction experts made boxes.

The librarians organized books.

"William's not helping," Jamaika told Mrs. McBee.

"Give him time, honey," Mrs. McBee said.

Jamaika huffed.

The packers filled the boxes.

The spellers labeled them.

And the movers lined them up.

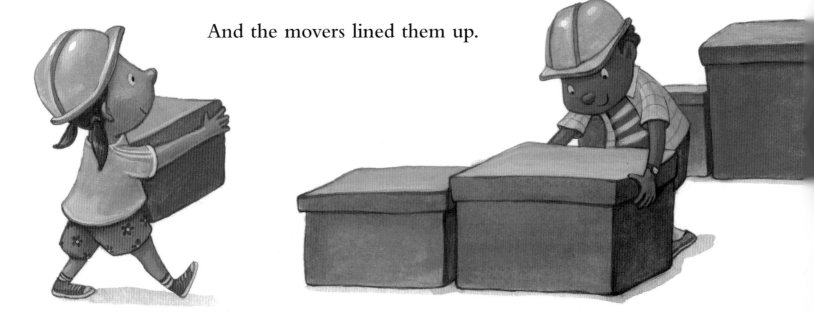

"William's not helping," Jamaika complained.

"He'll come around," said Mrs. McBee.

Jamaika huffed again. Louder.

The animal experts released the walking sticks and the butterflies outside.

They found the missing mouse and carried it back to its whirly-wheel in the library.

"William's still not helping," Jamaika reported again.

"He's working on it," said Mrs. McBee.

Jamaika huffed as loud as a hurricane.

When all the boxes were closed and
labeled and carted away, the children looked
around Room 3.

They frowned.

"It's so empty," said Max.

"It's lonely," said Lou.

"It's sad," Flora sighed.

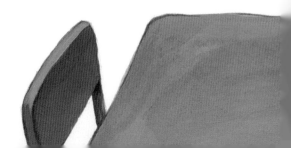

"I can't remember what it used
to look like!" Jamaika cried.

Mrs. McBee gathered them close. "Children, this is called a bittersweet moment. It's like swirly ice cream with sad and happy twisted together. We're sad about saying good-bye, but we're happy about what's ahead."

"Like playing all day!"

"And swimming!"

"And camping!"

"And reading!" said Mrs. McBee.

"But when summer is over, we'll be back here," Flora said. "Without you."

"That's true," said Mrs. McBee. "But you'll be excited about meeting your new teacher and making new friends in a brand new grade. And you'll have each other too."

In the silence that followed, she said,

"Thank you all for helping today."

Jamaika whipped her arm through the air.
"William didn't help," she protested.

"Where is that William?" Mrs. McBee asked.

Jamaika shrugged and pointed to the big lumpy
bag at the front of the room. "Mrs. McBee, you
still haven't shown us what's left in there."

"Everything, Jamaika, in its own sweet time,"
said Mrs. McBee.

Just then, the custodian carted one box back

into Room 3. It was marked *To Mrs. McBee*.

It wiggled.

Mrs. McBee lifted the lid. A yellow hard hat
popped up like a jack-in-the-box.

"Hi, William," said Mrs. McBee.

Jamaika stomped her foot. "See! All
William did was play all day!"

Mrs. McBee asked, "Is that true, William?"

He shook his head. Then he held out a stack
of pictures for everyone to see.

The children gathered around William and his pictures.

"There's Mrs. McBee playing her guitar," said Flora.

"And us reading," said Max and Lou.

"And Room 3 the way it used to be," Jamaika sighed.

"Mrs. McBee!" Jamaika said. "William was helping all along! He was helping us remember!"

"I know," said Mrs. McBee. "Every one of you has your own special way of helping. Just as every one of you has your own way of saying good-bye." She knocked on the top of William's hardhat and smiled.

"I made something else," William said. "But you have to close your eyes."

Mrs. McBee squeezed her eyes shut tight.

"No peeking," Jamaika said.

All the kids signed William's card.

"You can look now!" the children told Mrs. McBee.

Mrs. McBee held the card close. "This is beautiful!" she said softly. "But I wasn't the only one who made Room 3 special. It was all of us, together, helping each other grow. Room 3 needed the special magic of each and every one of you."

She opened her arms wide. "It's time for a McBeehive hug," she said.

The custodian, the principal, and the lunch ladies joined in the hug too.

And they topped off the day with swirly ice cream cones.